SNOW WHITE AND THE WICKED WITCH

SNOW WHITE AND THE WICKED WITCH

J.B. HARLAN

Copyright © 2025 by J.B. Harlan
All rights reserved. No part of this book may be reproduced in any manner whatsoever without written permission except in the case of brief quotations embodied in critical articles and reviews.
First Printing, 2025

Contents

Snow White and the Wicked Witch　　2
Gretel and Hansel　　26
The Velvet Ribbon　　41

SNOW WHITE
AND THE
WICKED WITCH

1

Snow White and the Wicked Witch

Once upon a time, in a kingdom cloaked by forests dark and wild, there lived a queen who longed for a child.

Though she prayed to the heavens and sought counsel from the wise, her womb remained barren, and her heart grew heavy. One winter's evening, as the first snow fell, she sat by her chamber window, and made a terrible vow.

"Let the snow take my blood," she whispered, "Let it drink my offering, and if it will grant me a child, I care not the cost."

She took a small dagger, and drew it across her palm. The crimson drops fell like rubies from the windowsill, hungrily swallowed by the snow. The white turned red, then black, and for a moment, she thought the snow shifted just a bit, though no wind stirred the air.

Days passed, and the queen began to feel the stirrings of life within her. But the joy she felt was sharp and fleeting, for her dreams were plagued by visions of a barefoot child walking on frozen ground, near black trees that wept blood. Yet when she woke, drenched in sweat, she dismissed the dreams as foolishness, and caressed the scar across her palm, for at last, her deepest wish had been fulfilled.

But as the months dragged on, the queen's health began to wane. Her skin became ashen, her voice grew weak, and the spark of life in her eyes dimmed away. The midwives whispered among themselves, for they had never seen a pregnancy so strange.

When the child finally came, it was in the dead of night, beneath a blood moon. The queen screamed once, twice, then fell silent as the babe emerged. The midwives delivered the child with trembling hands - a girl with a tuft of silver hair atop her tiny head, as pale as the frost that drank her mother's blood. The queen, now lifeless, lay with her face turned toward the window, her lips frozen in a faint smile as the sun began to rise.

As the grief-stricken king looked upon his newborn daughter, he declared the child's name to be Snow White. And the beautiful baby sat there in the morning sunlight, the perfect child they'd always wanted; and it was summer - warm, beautiful summer.

The child grew, and with each passing year, her beauty became more unnatural. The servants whispered that she never cried as a babe, not even when the winter winds howled like starving wolves. Instead, she would stare silently, or smile charmingly, and steal away the hearts of those whose lucky eyes greeted her.

But not all who saw Little Snow White were bewitched by the young girl's shimmering eyes and smile. Eventually, the King took himself another wife - a woman of breathtaking beauty, with flawless features sharp enough to cut glass, and a regal bearing that commanded the very air around her.

She had no love for the king, nor for the kingdom she now ruled. Her only passion was her own reflection, which she gazed upon in a mirror of polished obsidian, its surface as dark and impenetrable as her soul. The ancient looking glass was framed in blackened gold adorned with twisting serpents with red eyes.

Every morning, the queen stood before it, looked at herself, and said, "Mirror, mirror, on the wall, who is the fairest of the land?"

To this the mirror answered, "You, my queen, are fairest of all."

And she was satisfied, for she knew that the mirror could only speak the truth.

Time passed, and from the moment she could walk, Snow White enchanted all who laid eyes upon her. Her shining hair gleamed even on the grayest of days, and though untouched by time, remained the purest shade of fresh-fallen snow under a winter moon. Her skin was perfect, and luminous, and her plumping lips the color of ripe cherries.

Servants paused their work to marvel at her. Foreigners brought tales of her beauty back to their lands, claiming no other princess could compare. But the wicked queen's mirror, the only reflecting surface she permitted in the castle, was poison to all eyes but her own.

The handsome King, a man of noble bearing and strong features, would look into the glass to see a hideous ogre staring back at him, and little Snow White, beautiful and perfect as she was, saw a pale, deathly girl in the mirror, gaunt and hollow-eyed, and it filled her with horrible dread.

"Stepmother!" Snow White would cry. "I hate the sight of my own reflection so much. One day, I hope to be as beautiful as you."

The queen's lips curved into a smile though it did not reach her eyes. "Perhaps one day, after I am long gone," she said, her voice low and honeyed with false warmth, "you will be the prettiest in all the land."

But her stepmother could not bear the adoration that Snow White received, nor how the air seemed to brighten in her presence, and every smile and sneaking glance became a thorn in her side, and her hatred of the little girl grew with every passing day. The young girl's beauty was not hers to control, and this truth, more than any, festered in her heart like a venomous rot.

At night, the queen would stand before the mirror, curling her claws around its gilded frame. Her reflection looked back at her, beautiful and unyielding - but that was no longer enough.

"Mirror on the wall," she would ask, "who is the fairest of the land?"

The mirror's surface rippled like pooled ink as it said, "You, my queen, are fair; it is true. But Snow White is a thousand times fairer than you."

"Snow White!" the woman spat the name like poison from her tongue, clenching her fists so angrily that her long nails drew blood. "Snow White."

And in the darkness of her chamber, the wicked queen began to plot.

One day, Snow White came to her stepmother with wildflowers, her hair catching the golden light of the throne room as she approached. "Stepmother," she said innocently, "I picked these for you."

The queen accepted the flowers, her fingers brushing against Snow White's for the briefest of moments. "How lovely," she said through her jaw clenched so tightly, it ached.

Snow White curtsied and turned away, skipping toward the gardens once more as her laughter rang through the air like windchimes. The queen watched her go, her chest heaving with suppressed hatred, and the flowers withered and blackened in her grasp.

The following day, the queen summoned a huntsman to her chambers, a broad-shouldered man weathered by years of labor across the lands, with hands thickly calloused from wielding axe and knife.

She commanded him to take Snow White out into the woods. "Kill her, and to prove that you've done it, bring me her heart."

The huntsman's loyalty to the crown was unwavering, but still, he hesitated, for Snow White was just more than a child, innocent and kind. But he dared not disobey, for the queen was renowned for her wrath, so he bowed his head and left the queen alone with her dark thoughts.

She traced her fingers over her own face in the magic mirror. "A pure heart," she whispered to herself, "untouched by wickedness, untouched by sin."

The queen reached into her vanity and drew forth an ancient tome, its leather cover cracked with age, its pages yellowed and brittle. She turned to a page marked with a blood-red ribbon, and read the jagged script, in some long-forgotten language older than the castle itself:

"Eat of the heart, and youth shall return, as does spring after winter snow. The flesh will mend, the soul will thrive, and beauty reigns eternal."

Her hands trembled as she closed the book, the weight of its promise filling her chest with dark delight. She imagined her face restored to its most youthful beauty, her essence surpassing even that of the gods. Snow White, with her cursed hair, would be the vessel of her rebirth.

"Soon," she hissed, "I shall be fairest of all."

The next day, the huntsman led Snow White deep into the woods, beyond the sunlight, where the trees grew taller, and a chill settled in the air, though it was not the chill of winter.

At last, they reached a clearing, and the huntsman turned to face the girl.

"Why have we come here, Huntsman?" she asked when they reached a barren clearing, her voice as soft as a bird's song.

"Forgive me, Princess," he said, drawing his knife.

Snow White stepped back, her small hands raised. "Please," she pleaded, her voice trembling. "Don't hurt me."

For a moment, the knife faltered in his hand, and before he could decide, Snow White darted into the woods, her feet light as a doe's. She ran blindly, branches clawing at her arms and face, the gnarled roots rising to trip her.

Behind her, the huntsman shouted, his voice growing louder as he closed the distance. Spying a fallen branch thick with moss, she snatched it up and hid behind a tree, her small frame trembling as she listened to his heavy footfalls approaching.

When he appeared, she leaped from the shadows with a cry, swinging the branch with all her strength. It struck him squarely in the side of the head, and he stumbled, falling to his knees. The knife fell from his hand, skittering across the forest floor to the small feet of Snow White.

The huntsman looked up at her, his face streaked with dirt. "Spare me," he begged, his voice breaking. "Spare me as I would have spared you."

Snow White stood over him, her chest heaving. "Leave me be, then," she said, dropping the branch. "Go, and never come for me again."

But before the huntsman could rise, thick black vines shot forth from the forest, wrapping around his legs and arms. He screamed as they tightened, struggling to free himself, but it was no use.

The earth itself had come to claim him, dragging him violently across the forest floor. Thorny tendrils snagged and lurched, ripping into his pores and snaking into his veins.

Snow White dared one final glance over her shoulder as she fled. The huntsman's broken body dangled high among the branches like a tangled marionette, his face locked forever in a silent scream.

Then a great hawk descended, and with a sudden, violent motion, plunged its talons into the huntsman's chest, and tore out his heart, before taking to the sky once again with a piercing cry, leaving a trail of blood below.

The queen in her chambers turned sharply at the sound of a soft thud upon her dressing table. There, amid her perfumes and jewels, lay a fresh human heart, still slick with dark blood. She stared at it glistening in the dim light, and her lips parted in thrill.

"At last," she whispered, her hands trembling as she reached for the organ. It was still warm as she pressed it to her lips. "At last, I shall have her heart."

The queen called for a servant, and bade him visit the king's chambers with the dreadful news of his young daughter's death in the forest. As the servant departed, she turned her gaze to the hearth, where a small cauldron bubbled, and carefully placed the meat into the broth. She sprinkled a handful of salt crystals like snow onto the organ, and with a bone-handled ladle, she stirred the concoction. The gurgling stew filled the room with the metallic scents of death and despair, and the queen watched it simmer as low hunger rumbled in the pit of her stomach.

"Beauty eternal," she murmured, ladling out the tender and steaming heart onto a shining golden plate. She used a silver knife to cut into the flesh. The meat was soft, rich and succulent, almost sickly sweet, and the wicked queen savored each bite with her eyes half-closed in ecstasy, until the plate was as spotless as her own visage.

She leaned back in her chair, her laughter echoing through the stone halls. "Snow White is no more," she said to herself. "And I am, once again, the fairest of them all."

Meanwhile, deep in the forest, far across the kingdom, the poor princess ran on without daring to look back. Just as her legs threatened to give way, she saw a small figure ahead—no, not a figure, but a house. A little cottage, barely more than a silhouette against the darkening sky. Its thatched roof sagged slightly, and its wooden walls were weathered and worn, and Snow White carried herself, numb with exhaustion, to the little front door.

Her small fist rapped against the wood three times, and she waited, but no answer came. She knocked again, louder this time, her voice cracking as she called out, "Please, is anyone there?"

Still, there was no reply.

With no other choice, she pushed open the door. The room inside was dim and cold. A small table stood in the center, covered with a snow white cloth that looked as if it had never known a stain. Seven little plates sat upon it, each with a spoon resting neatly beside it, and seven knives and forks, and seven mugs. Against the far wall, seven little beds stood in perfect formation, each one covered with blankets smooth and untouched.

Snow White hesitated, but her hunger outweighed her unease. She moved to the table and took a small piece of bread from each plate, and nibbled on a few vegetables, and drank a small sip of wine from each mug.

When she finished, and her eyelids fluttered with drowsiness, she moved to the beds. The first bed was too long, the second too sunken-in, and the third was too soft. It wasn't until she reached the seventh bed that she found one just right.

The cool blankets soon warmed around her as she curled into a ball, spilling her silver hair across the pillow, and she closed her eyes, drifting off to sleep.

After dark, the masters of the house returned home. They were seven little men who mined for ore in the mountains. They filled the cottage one by one and lit their seven candles, when one said: "Who has sat in my chair?"

Then a second voice cried, "Who has sipped from my mug?"

Then a third, and a fourth, until all seven shouted!

"Who has eaten my vegetables?"

"Who has eaten my bread?"

"Who has touched my plate?"

"...my fork?"

"...my knife?"

And there, lying in the seventh bed, was the girl, her chest rising and falling with each quiet breath, her hair, as white as freshly fallen snow, spread across the pillow like a soft, frozen veil.

The dwarfs cried out in amazement. Such an ethereal beauty had appeared from nowhere, asleep in their home, and they could hardly believe their eyes. They gathered around the bed, their candles casting golden light over her.

"Who is she?" one of the little men whispered.

"Where did she come from?" asked another.

"She looks like a princess," murmured a third. "But what is a princess doing here in our cottage?"

The fourth man shook his head. "No matter the reason, we musn't disturb her."

And so they left her there in the seventh bed, and the seventh dwarf would sleep with his companions, switching beds every hour, until the sun came.

The next morning Snow White awoke, and when she saw the seven dwarfs, she was frightened. But they were friendly, with faces that were kind and curious, and one of them asked her name.

The princess sat up, clutching the blanket to her chest. "I am Snow White," she said softly. Then she told them that her stepmother had tried to kill her, and that she had run the entire day, finally coming to their house.

The dwarfs said, "If you will cook, make the beds, wash, sew, and knit, and keep everything clean and orderly, then you can stay with us, and you shall have everything that you want."

"Yes," said Snow White, "with all my heart."

Far away, in the cold stone halls of the castle, the queen awoke that morning feeling strange. Surely the effects of her wicked meal had manifested, and she rose from her bed, eager to see her beauty restored and youth renewed.

But when she stood before the magic mirror, disgust filled her heart. The face that stared back at her was sallow and sunken, deeply marked by lines of age and pocked with craters.

She had been deceived. The princess had outwitted her. The heart she had consumed was not Snow White's.

A terrible fury rose within the queen, and her scream echoed through the castle halls. When her servant appeared, the queen beckoned him to summon the king, for she would command him to speak of her beauty, to affirm her perfection, as she had done countless times before.

But the servant did not move with the usual haste; instead, he looked at her grimly, his face pale with sorrow. "My queen," he began, "upon hearing of Snow White's passing in the forest, the King succumbed to grief too great to bear."

The queen stood in silence, the weight of her deeds heavier than the crown upon her brow. "A mistake," she hissed.

But the servant was steadfast. "His heart shattered, my queen. Our great King has passed into death's embrace."

The queen's breath caught in her throat, and the servant lingered before he bowed his head and retreated.

When she was alone, the wicked woman crossed to the magic mirror, and said, "Mirror on the wall, where is that filthy little stain on the world, Snow White?"

The mirror's surface began to ripple, and the reflection shifted to form an image of a cottage nestled deep in the forest, and inside the little glowing windows sat Snow White, her hair as pale as a winter corpse, her face serene and untouched.

A scream tore from the queen's throat, like the howl of a wounded beast. "No!" she gasped, her voice rising to a shriek of fury. She slammed her fist against the glass and stumbled backwards, gasping for air. A jagged crack had formed upon the glass, and as her hand flew to her face, the queen left a smear of blood across her cheek.

She would not be thwarted by that little brat. She would not be humiliated by a child! And she would not rely on others to do her bidding any longer.

Coloring her face with paints and powders, the queen disguised herself as an old seamstress. She donned a long cloak, and filled a basket with little trinkets and fabrics, and made her way to the house of the seven dwarfs, where she knocked upon the door and called out in a voice like dry leaves, "Beautiful wares for sale, for sale!"

Snow White, hearing the voice from the window, peeked out. "Good day, dear woman, what do you have for sale?"

"Colorful silk corsets," the old woman croaked, pulling from the folds of her tattered cloak a lace so delicate it shimmered like a spider's web. "This one would suit you perfectly, little girl. Would you like it?"

Snow White, innocent and trusting, thought only of the trinkets the woman offered. *How kind she must be,* she thought, as she unbolted the door and stepped outside.

"Child," the witch cackled, "how delicate you are! Let me lace you up properly." She stepped closer, and before Snow White could speak, the old woman wrapped the lace around the girl's waist, pulling so violently that Snow White gasped, her breath cut short.

The silk tightened, choking her more with every tug, as the old woman laughed and laughed. With one final, vicious yank, the lace drew deathly tight, and Snow White crumpled to the ground, lifeless before the door.

The queen stood over her, her lips curled into a grim smile as she looked down at the girl, "At last, all eyes in the kingdom shall belong to me again."

Not long afterward, the seven men came home. How terrified they were when they saw their dear Snow White lying on the ground, not moving at all. They lifted her up, and, seeing that she was too tightly laced, they cut the lace in two. Then, faintly, she began to breathe again, and little by little, she came back to life.

When the wicked queen returned to her castle, she went straight to her mirror, certain that her rival was gone, and she herself would be named the fairest of them all.

"Mirror on the wall," she asked, "who is the fairest of the land?"

The mirror answered once again: "You, my queen, are fair; it is true. But Snow White, Is still a thousand times fairer than you."

When she heard that, all her blood ran to her heart. "This time," she said, "I shall think of something that will destroy her once and for all."

With the dark art of witchcraft, the queen forged a comb of poisoned ivory, and wrapped herself in another disguise, this time as a peddler woman. When she arrived at the little house, she knocked, as she called, "Good wares for sale, for sale!"

Snow White, peering from the window, said, "Go on your way. I am not allowed to let anyone in."

But the wicked woman smiled, and said with a croon, "Surely you may take a look."

Then she pulled out the poisoned comb, its sharp, gleaming teeth catching the light, and the child, too trusting and too innocent, saw the comb and admired its delicate craftsmanship, and without further hesitation, opened the door.

"Now, let me comb your hair properly," the queen said in a voice low and sweet, and before Snow White could realize the danger, the old woman thrust it into her hair.

The cold fangs of the comb sank into her scalp, and the effect was instant. Snow White's eyes fluttered, and within moments, she collapsed to the floor.

"Now you are finished," said the wicked witch. And she turned and walked away, her ragged cloak billowing behind her like a shadow, leaving Little Snow White lifeless on the ground.

Fortunately, it was almost evening, and the seven dwarfs soon returned home. When they saw Snow White lying on the ground as if she were dead, they examined her and found the poisoned comb tangled in her hair. They had scarcely pulled it out when Snow White's eyes fluttered, and she came to herself once again.

"What happened?" she whispered sweetly.

"You were poisoned," said the eldest man. And once again they warned her never to open the door for anyone.

Back at the castle, the queen stepped before her mirror and said, "Mirror on the wall, who is the fairest of the land?"

When the queen heard the mirror's answer, she shrieked like an animal in its death throes, and swore, "Snow White shall die if it costs me my life!"

Then she went into her most secret room and fashioned a poisoned apple. From the outside it was beautiful, white with red cheeks, and anyone who saw it would want it. But a single taste of its flesh would bring death.

The witch colored her face, and disguised herself as a fruit seller, and set out across the seven mountains for the little cottage in the woods.

Upon hearing a knock at the door, Snow White stuck her head out the window and said, "I am not allowed to let anyone in."

"That is all right with me," answered the woman. "Here, I'll give you an apple through the window."

"No, thank you," said Snow White, "I cannot accept anything."

"Are you afraid of poison?" asked the old woman. "Look, I'll cut the apple in two. You eat the red half, and I shall eat the white half."

Snow White longed for the beautiful apple, and when she saw that the woman was eating part of it, she could no longer resist. So she stuck her hand out and took the other half of the fruit, which had been so artfully made that only the red half was deathly, and Snow White had barely taken a bite when she fell to the ground dead.

The queen looked at her with a gruesome stare, laughed loudly, and said, "This time no one can awaken you."

Back at the castle, the magic mirror finally answered, "You, my queen, are fairest of all."

And her envious heart was at rest.

When the dwarfs came home, Snow White was dead. They lifted her up and looked for something poisonous. They undid her laces. They combed her hair. They washed her with water and wine. But nothing helped. The dear princess was gone.

They laid her on a platform, and sat next to her and mourned for three days. Then, they were going to bury her, but she still had her beautiful red cheeks, and looked as fresh as a living person.

Instead, they had a transparent glass coffin made, so she could be seen from all sides. They laid her inside, and with golden letters inscribed on it her name, and that she was a princess. Then they put the coffin outside on a mountain, and one of them always stayed with it and watched over her.

Now it came to pass that a prince entered these woods, and he happened upon the coffin on the mountain with beautiful Snow White in it, and he read what was written in golden letters.

His heart filled with sorrow and admiration upon seeing her breathtaking beauty. Then he said to the dwarfs, "Let me have the coffin. I will give you anything you want for it."

But the dwarfs answered, "We will not sell it for all the gold in the world."

"Then give it to me," said the prince, "for I cannot live without being able to see Snow White's beauty, her rosy cheeks and frosty hair. I will honor her and respect her as my most cherished one."

As he thus spoke, the good dwarfs felt pity for him, and gave him the coffin. The prince had his servants carry it away on their shoulders. But one of them stumbled on some brush, and this dislodged from Snow White's throat the piece of poisoned apple that she had bitten off.

Not long afterward, she opened her eyes, lifted the lid from her coffin, sat up, and was alive again. "Good heavens!" she cried out "Where am I?"

The prince, overcome with joy, told her what had happened, and asked for her hand in marriage, and together, they went to his father's castle, and their wedding was planned with great majesty.

Snow White's godless stepmother was invited to the feast, and her vanity could not resist the opportunity to show herself in all her finery. She dressed in her most beautiful clothes and glistening jewels, and stood before her mirror.

"Mirror on the wall," she said, "who is the fairest in the land?"

The mirror answered, "Your reign has ended, try as you might, the prince's true love is one Little Snow White."

The witch uttered a curse, and without thinking, seized a nearby candlestick and swung it at the mirror. The glass shattered like thunder, scattering across the room, and the mirror, her longtime faithful servant, was in ruins. Her reflection was gone.

The wicked witch did not want to go to the wedding. But she knew she had to see the young queen for herself, to confirm the mirror's terrible truth. And so, she began to plot her final act of vengeance.

She took a pair of iron shoes, heavy and crude, and bewitched them so they appeared light and pretty, their laces delicate as snowflakes. But once worn, their true nature would be revealed.

She planned to present them as a wedding gift, but without her magic mirror, the queen's attempts to alter her appearance were clumsy and ineffective. In the end, she buried herself in layers of fabric, and hunched over so far that she was practically horizontal, and headed for the celebration dressed as a beggar woman.

When she arrived at the wedding, the guards barred her way, and the wicked witch wept with feigned sorrow. "Please," she begged, "I raised Little Snow White from a baby. I shan't miss her wedding day. It would break my heart."

The guards exchanged uneasy glances as Snow White herself appeared at the gate, radiant in her wedding gown.

"Who are you?" the sweet bride asked gently, eying the hunched figure before her.

The witch bowed her head, "I have traveled far to see you on this joyous day. I am but a poor woman who once cared for you, my dear."

Snow White's memory failed to place the woman, but her kindness outweighed her suspicion.

"Let her in," she said to the guards. "It is a day of celebration, and no one should be turned away."

The guards stepped aside, and the witch shuffled into the castle. She attempted to give Snow White the shoes right away. "My dear," she sang, "I have brought you a wedding gift. These shoes will make you the most graceful dancer in the land."

But Snow White gently shook her head. "Thank you, but let us wait until the first dance. I would not want to spoil the surprise."

The witch nodded, her hands tightening around the shoes. She would have to wait, but not for long.

Meanwhile, the dwarfs, who had also been invited to the wedding, watched the old woman with sharp eyes, and when they saw the shoes in her hands, they recognized the work of witchcraft.

While the queen was distracted, they stole the cursed heels and threw them into the burning coals of the castle's hearth, hoping to destroy them. But the shoes did not burn.

The grand ballroom filled with music and laughter when the newlywed couple made their entrance after the ceremony. The wicked witch, her patience worn thin, could wait no longer. She pushed her way to the center of the floor, her voice rising above the music.

"Servants!" she called, her tone sharp and commanding. "Bring Snow White her dancing shoes! She must wear them for the first dance!"

The room fell silent, and Snow White looked at the woman, and the dwarfs stepped forward, gripping the red-hot dancing shoes with large tongs.

"These are no gift for a bride," the eldest man declared. "They have been cursed to bring her harm."

Before the queen could react, the seven dwarfs surrounded her, taking hold of her limbs and thrusting the shoes onto her feet. Her burning flesh sizzled and smoked as the iron seared her skin, and the witch filled the hall with screams of agony.

The cursed shoes forced her to dance, their black magic forcing her body into frantic, uncontrollable spins. Round and round she whirled, her screams echoing through the ballroom, as the heat of the iron burned deeper, and the stench of charred flesh filled the air. Yet still the wicked witch danced.

The woman's horrible, twisted face, and terrible, ungodly cries, began to thaw away Snow White's buried past, and soon, she knew exactly who the beggar woman was. "Stepmother," she whispered.

Finally, with one last, horrible screech, the witch collapsed to the floor, where she lay shuddering, her charred feet unable to carry her further. The guests gaped in horror at the fallen queen, and the hall was silent, save for the crackling of the fire and the faint hiss of the cooling iron.

Snow White stepped forward with sorrowful eyes, as shimmering snowflakes began to flutter around her like little bees with wings of frost. The guests gasped in awe, and whispered with wonder, as Snow White reached out towards the smoldering witch's form, and her little frozen workers snuffed the flames like a candle.

"Let this be an end to her cruelty," she said softly. "May she find peace in death, as we have found peace in life."

After a brief and joyous honeymoon, Snow White and her prince returned to their new castle, their hearts light with happiness. The dwarfs, ever loyal, arrived soon after, carrying Snow White's old belongings from the wicked queen's castle.

Then Snow White, with eyes bright as morning dew, smiled and spoke thus: "You have ever been my true family, and it is only right that you no longer dwell in such a humble space. I know of a grand castle, at last empty of its cruel queen, where far more than seven bedchambers stand waiting, and more than seven of every dish lie unused. If it pleases you, dear friends, take it as your own, and let its halls ring with laughter once more."

The dwarfs looked upon one another with wide, joyous eyes, and a great cheer rose from their throats. In a flurry of excitement, they hurried off to cross the seven mountains and gather their humble belongings from the little cottage that had served them so well.

As Snow White sifted through the remnants of her past, her fingers brushed against something cold and jagged. There, half-buried in the dusty trinkets, lay the broken frame of the magic mirror. She lifted it gently, and touched the broken frame, and in that instant, a chill swept through the air, not of winter, but something older, something ancient.

A sleek layer of ice began to form before her eyes, shimmering faintly like frost on a winter's morn, and soon, the mirror's surface was perfection again.

For the first time, Snow White saw her true reflection, not just of her face, but her very soul. She was no longer the girl who had fled into the woods. She was a queen. And she stood there in the morning sunlight, grown up but a child at heart; and it was summer - warm, beautiful summer.

GRETEL AND HANSEL

2

Gretel and Hansel

Once upon a time in a small village, there lived a poor woodcutter and his wife.

They had two children, a girl named Gretel, and a boy named Hansel. The boy had his father's blue eyes and darker features, while the girl inherited her mother's bright green eyes and blond hair. Despite the woodcutter's best efforts to provide for his family, they struggled to make ends meet.

One day, the woodcutter's wife hatched a sinister plan. She suggested that they take the children deep into the woods and abandon them. "We'd have twice the food," she said, "and twice the drink, and twice the room!"

The woodcutter was horrified by his wife's suggestion and refused to go along with it. But as time passed, the family's struggles grew more dire, and the woodcutter's wife became more and more insistent on her plan. The family was sickly and thin, and it was only a matter of time before they'd start to perish.

One night, when the woodcutter was out chopping wood, the desperate mother took matters into her own hands. She sneaked into the children's room and whispered to them that they were going to take a walk in the woods. They would pick special berries that you could only see by the light of the moon. She promised them a great adventure and an overflowing bounty. After handing each child a small piece of bread, she led them deep into the woods, taunting that they'd find the berries soon.

"There they are!" she exclaimed. "Just ahead! Run straight away and fill your baskets with as many berries as you can!"

Terribly hungry and filled with excitement, the children took off through the dark trees, eager to find the special berries. But as they looked around, there were none to be found, and they soon realized that their mother hadn't followed.

Gretel and Hansel were horribly afraid of the woods at night, and had made no attempt to keep track of their path. They called for their mother, but she didn't respond, and eventually, they gave up. The children huddled together underneath a tree until the first signs of the sun.

In the chilly morning light, they began to find their way home again.

"I hope mother is alright," said Gretel, pushing aside a limb to let her brother pass under. "She never was dependable with directions."

Hansel turned back with a solemn look on his face. "I think she's been snatched up by a bear."

"Hansel!" Gretel snapped.

"If not something worse," he continued.

Suddenly, a small shelter came into view. It barely stood out from the trees around it, and was nearly a mirror image of their own home, other than one noticeable difference.

"Is that our cottage?" Hansel asked.

"Don't be silly, Hansel," Gretel said. "We don't have a chimney!"

"Whoever it is, maybe they'll give us something to eat!" Hansel said as his eyes widened.

"And maybe they'll help us find our way home!" Gretel added.

Giggling, the children took off in a sprint towards the cottage, banging on the door and asking to be let inside.

A mysterious old woman opened the heavy wooden door, with frizzy gray hair and a long black cloak. She spoke with a raspy voice that was not unkind, and invited the children inside to grow warm by the fire.

After some time had passed, the woman called the children to sit at the table, where a massive feast had appeared. They saw roasted potatoes, carrots, and asparagus in shades of green and purple. Clouds of steam danced romantically above a glistening turkey and several small hens, each accompanied by a wooden bowl overflowing with fresh leafy green salads with boiled eggs, candied nuts, sweet-but-tart dried berries and freshly-milked goat cheese, all decadently swirled with velvety balsamic glaze. Proudly at the center was a full pig with an apple in its mouth.

Even better, there were pastries, chocolates, fairy cakes, and puddings. The children saw trees made of licorice, and gingerbread houses. Truffles, and tarts, and marzipan horses sat beside a mountain of buttery caramel apples, each dazzling with glistening sprinkles and chocolate chips.

Gretel and Hansel filled plate after plate, eating as much as they could until they fell asleep on their plates.

In the morning, the children awoke by the fire with no memory of moving to the floor. They were covered in heavy quilts and fought the urge to sleep the day away. Finding them awake, the old woman surprised the children with beautiful clean clothes that were just the right sizes, and another feast for breakfast.

As the days went by, Gretel and Hansel grew more and more comfortable in the cottage. They were well-fed, and the woman taught them how to weave baskets, plant a garden, and bake delicious desserts. For a time, they almost forgot about their parents back home.

On a stormy evening some weeks later, Gretel awoke by the fire. The sounds of strange whispers had pulled her from her slumber, coming from behind the locked door of the old woman's private quarters. The raspy voice was quite familiar, but Gretel couldn't understand any of the words.

She tip-toed across the room, her eyes on the soft glow sneaking from the room underneath the doorway. There was a large keyhole in the door, and Gretel cautiously put her eye to it. Inside the room, the woman stood above an ancient book. She was moving her hands around fantastically, chanting what sounded to Gretel like gibberish. Most horrifying, the woman looked much older, meaner, and uglier than she ever had before, and Gretel knew immediately that they were staying in the house of a witch.

She returned to her quilt on the floor next to Hansel, and stared at the ceiling until the morning came.

Though the food was still delicious, the massive feasts had started to overwhelm the children, and the witch loved to remark about how plump they were getting. "You poor things were as thin as strings!" she said, "But my delicious meals will fatten you right up." The smile on her face faded ominously as she stared intently at Hansel, and she said in a low voice, "I could just eat you."

A few days later, as the children gathered wood for the fire, Gretel admitted her fears to her brother for the first time. She told him that the woman must be an ancient witch, and her powers were fading in front of them.

"So what if she's a witch!" Hansel cried. "I'll never go back to living of stale bread and water. We have a warm place to live now, Gretel, with all the food we could want."

"There are always consequences for reaping the benefits of dark magic," she reminded him. "Didn't you listen to a single one of father's stories?"

The mention of their father stung him. Hansel was so enamored by the life of excess offered by the witch that he'd almost forgotten what his own parents looked like. "I can barely remember him now," he said distantly.

"Hansel, I think that's because of her. I think she needs to use us to strengthen her powers and hide her true appearance. I think she's preparing for something."

"Preparing for what?" he asked, fear on full display in his eyes. "If we don't get away from here," she said, "I think she's planning to eat us."

The children devised their plan as they walked back to the cottage, arms overflowing with sticks and twigs. They'd offer to clean the home meticulously to thank the woman for her graciousness, and hopefully buy the chance for Gretel to steal a glance at the woman's book.

"What well-mannered children you are!" the woman cried when they offered their help. "And today's the perfect day. We're having something special for dinner, and I need to fetch some herbs from the forest."

"Oh, please!" Hansel exclaimed, nearly salivating. "What are we having?"

The woman smiled at him menacingly. She, too, was nearly salivating. "It's a surprise."

As the woman set off into the forest, Hansel scrubbed the kitchen as instructed, and Gretel pulled the ring of keys hanging on the wall. Trying each one, she finally felt the satisfying jolt of the door unlocking, and pushed it open cautiously.

The book was right before her on the table. It looked ancient, tattered, and worn with use. As Gretel cautiously flipped the pages, she noticed countless different languages, and handwriting from more hands than she could count. She lost track of time staring at the book, trying to understand the recipes and spells before her. And finally, she found it.

Though she couldn't decipher the text, the crude drawings were clear enough. They depicted a haggard old woman with a large cauldron. The next image showed the woman holding a baby, and then, the baby inside the cauldron. The final image depicted no baby at all, but the woman was now young and beautiful.

Tearing the page from the book, Gretel sprinted to the door, but was shocked to find it locked from the outside. "Hansel!" she yelled. "The door is stuck! Let me out!"

But Hansel didn't reply. Instead, she heard the most horrible, grating, terrible cackling laughter. The witch had returned.

"Hansel! Answer me!" Gretel cried, banging on the wood with all her might.

"He's busy, my dear," the witch responded in a sing-song voice. "But supper will be ready soon."

Weeping, Gretel glanced around the room for anything that could help her open the door. Only now did she notice the window high on the wall in the back of the room.

Quickly, she pulled various items together to create a makeshift staircase and climbed her way to the window. The shutter loudly squeaked as she opened it outwards, and she froze with fear as she waited to see if she'd been caught. But she heard nothing.

With a deep breath, she hoisted herself through the window, landing with a painful thud in the grass below. Wincing, she pulled herself to her feet and turned towards the door.

She was face to face with the hideous witch.

Gretel awoke tied to a chair at the table. The rough ropes were tight and chafed away at her skin, and her ankles were bound to the wooden legs.

"Welcome back," the witch said as she placed a steaming bowl on the table. "I'm so glad you could join me for dinner."

Gretel's vision was foggy, but she could smell another one of the witch's feasts before her.

"Where's my brother?" she spat. "What did you do to him?"

The witch laughed. "You know the answer to that, darling. I can see it on your face."

Gretel's vision was returning by the second, and she could make out the shape of the witch excitedly enjoying her meal. There was bread, and vegetables, and—

Gretel screamed louder than she ever had before. In the center of the table, she saw her younger brother.

He held an apple in his mouth.

Gretel convulsed, screaming and shaking, desperately trying to break away from the ropes, but it was no use. She wept, falling still in the chair as the witch enjoyed the meal in front of her.

"It's so delicious," the witch said, running her tongue up and down her greasy fingers before returning to the roast and carving away. "I know you must be hungry."

"I'll never eat anything from you ever again," Gretel hissed, "You're a disgusting, evil witch!"

"On second thought," the witch said as returned to her feet, "I think I'll feed you myself."

Gretel shook with fear as the woman walked towards her, her small feet seeming to land on the floor below with monstrously loud crashes. "No, please..." she cried, pulling against the ropes again in vain.

The witch's wrinkly hand landed on the table. She had long, overgrown nails hanging from the ends of her fingers, and she used one to stab a piece of meat. "You must have a taste, darling," the witch said with a horrifying grin as her finger neared Gretel's mouth.

The young girl tried to clench her jaw, but the witch used her other hand to plug her nose, and eventually, Gretel opened her mouth to gasp for air.

Without hesitation, the witch shoved her finger and the meat into Gretel's throat. "Eat it, you little shit! Eat your disgusting little brother!"

Gagging and choking for air, Gretel knew what she had to do. She bit down as hard as she could, and the witch screamed. Gretel bit harder and harder, clenching her jaw as the witch writhed around in agony, desperately attempting to pull her hand away from the girl's teeth. The girl could feel the bone cracking underneath the woman's frail skin. With a horrible cry, the witch slapped Gretel across the face with her free hand, and the force was strong enough to knock her over in the chair. But she didn't lessen the grip of her teeth, and with a slurping crunch, the witch's finger tore completely away from its hand.

The witch screamed and screamed in agony as Gretel spat the finger towards the fire. The witch dove for it, desperate to save her limb, as Gretel now realized the force of the fall had loosened the rope around her wrists.

As quickly as she could, she freed herself while the witch was distracted near the fire and tore into the woods. She knew the witch would be right behind her, and she had no idea where she was going.

She quickly arrived at a clearing, and looked around, eager to find a pathway towards help. But almost immediately, the witch arrived, too, and she was more furious than ever.

"You'll never escape me you little maggot!" she cried. Gretel could see that the woman's skin was bulging and stretching as if alive - the effects of the recipe were taking hold, and her body was attempting to rejuvenate itself. "I gave you everything you ever wanted," she hissed, "and now it's time you do the same for me."

The witch raised her hands in the air and began chanting once again. Mist grew from the forest floor and swirled around them. Just as the woman reached the finale of her incantation, Gretel revealed her secret: she had stolen the witch's book.

She quickly did her best to read the ancient text, sounding out the words before her as the witch came to realize what was happening. As the winds grew stronger and whipped through the trees, the witch attempted to make her way closer to the girl.

A fire, glowing blue and purple and green, came to life in the center of the clearing, its sparks joining the tornado of fog swirling around them.

Gretel could feel herself growing weaker. The witch's dark magic was sucking the life out of her. But she had nearly completed the spell of her own. She collapsed near the fire, feeling her lungs close in and her consciousness fade, as the witch cackled and cackled, and finally, in her loudest voice possible, Gretel completed the incantation.

But nothing happened.

As the witch began to cackle once again, the swirling sparks and mist began to settle, and the woman stood still, satisfied with herself. "Stupid girl," she hissed, looking down at her next meal. "That spell requires organic matter. Surely, you regret tossing my finger to the fire."

Fading fast, Gretel slowly formed a smirk with her lips, holding up the long, broken nail that had torn from the witch's finger.

Before the woman realized what was happening, Gretel flicked the nail into the flames, and the witch immediately screamed with agony. Her wrinkled skin erupted in the colorful blaze, turning from red to black before melting into the grass.

Gretel shielded her eyes as she felt her strength return. The witch was quickly overcome by the fire, collapsing to the ground before the girl and taking laboring breaths as she lived her final moments. Her hair had completely burned away, and her face appeared to melt like hot wax.

But Gretel was certain of one thing: she recognized the piercing green eyes looking back at her now. Her mother had been the witch all along.

"I will haunt you forever," the woman said breathlessly, "even in death."

Gretel stayed with her as she passed, unable to leave her own mother to die alone, and pushed the entire cursed book into the fire. It erupted with a tremendous boom, and then the book, and her mother, were gone.

The woodcutter had given up hope long ago that he'd ever see his children again, and when he saw Gretel emerge from the nearby trees, he couldn't believe his eyes. He ran towards her, openly weeping, and scooped her up into his arms.

"Father, I'm so sorry!" Gretel cried, burying her face in his strong chest and choking with sobs.

"It doesn't matter, my child," he promised, squeezing her tight. "You're back where you belong."

Gretel and her father feasted on everything in the house, and drank warm cider, and laughed and cried together.

She was worried he wouldn't believe what she said about her mother, but her father revealed that he, too, had been under the witch's spell.

The next morning, Gretel decided to go for a walk in search of fresh flowers to pick. But as she opened the cottage door, she nearly fainted. Sitting before her was the ancient, tattered book of spells, as if she'd never pushed it into the fire.

Gretel's heart beat like a drum. The book was calling to her, taunting her...

She bent down to pick it up, and the moment she touched it, the horrifying image of the cackling witch's face appeared before her, eyes glowing, mouth wide, and Gretel fell backward in shock.

After making certain that her father remained asleep, Gretel sneaked back to her bed and tucked the book underneath the mattress. It belonged to her now, and she could already feel the darkness creeping in.

"There are always consequences for reaping the benefits of dark magic..."

By using the witch's spell, Gretel had opened herself to its evil, planting an infection that would eventually overtake her completely. She could feel the lives of thousands of witches coming alive inside of her.

Gretel would be their vessel now.

And it felt good.

THE VELVET RIBBON

3

The Velvet Ribbon

It was love at first sight when Peter first laid his eyes on Melody.

He was walking his dog through the park on a crisp fall afternoon when they crossed paths. She wore a proper dress with puffed sleeves and a flower in her hair. Below her fashionable umbrella, a beautiful bracelet dangled from her wrist, and several rings decorated each hand. But most interesting was the black velvet ribbon tied around her neck, matching her hair, overflowing from her shoulders like spilled ink.

Melody felt the attention, and sent a smile Peter's way. That was all the invitation he needed to introduce himself. They spent the entire afternoon circling the park, and she allowed him to walk her home. They made plans to go to the theatre that weekend, and dinner the following evening.

Before they knew it, they were spending nearly all of their time together. Each day, she looked more beautiful than the last. And each day, she wore the black velvet ribbon around her neck. The rest of her adornments would come and go, but Peter never saw her without the ribbon. As she didn't acknowledge it, he hadn't mentioned it either. But every once in awhile, the curiosity became unbearable.

One evening, they were together in a beautiful restaurant. She wore an emerald green velvet dress with her hair pulled up into an elegant twist. On her head, she wore a small headpiece that contained both the green and black fabrics, seamlessly uniting her attire.

Finally, Peter felt close enough to his young love that he could inquire without offending. Placing his hand gently on hers, he finally asked the question that had been on his mind for so long. "Melody, my love. I don't mean to...may I ask why you wear the ribbon around your neck?"

Her face darkened before she quickly smiled, and shakily replied, "Oh, it's just something I've always worn. Don't you like it?"

"Of course I do!" he replied, "but I'd love to see your beautiful neck uncovered, my dear. Your sweet, soft skin..."

"I'm sorry, my love," she said, taking her hand from his. Then she ran the tips of her fingers along the fabric, as if consoling the ribbon itself...or confirming the bow remained tight.

"Then, will you tell me about it?" he asked.

The smile remained, but her eyes didn't sparkle. "There is nothing to tell."

In the days that followed, he desperately tried to stop thinking about the ribbon - but it ate away at him. He kept no secrets from his darling lover, yet there was something she refused to share. A part of her that remained unknown...

Shortly after they became engaged, a member of Peter's extended family passed away, and Melody left town with her partner to attend the funeral. They rented a room at a small inn, and for the first time, shared a bed. They kissed and cuddled by the light of the fire until they fell asleep.

In the morning, they were quietly packing their things when Melody timidly spoke, as if the words had weighed her down all morning. "My love...I'm afraid I slept quite terribly. I barely slept at all."

Peter was taken aback, as he'd slept soundly through the night. "I'm so sorry, dear. Did you not enjoy sharing the bed?"

"Oh, I loved falling asleep in your arms," she replied, "but I woke up in the middle of the night. I'd had such a terrible dream.

He could tell she was truly upset, and wrapped his arms around her as she continued.

"I was sleeping when I felt your fingers slide underneath my ribbon...trying to pull it off, picking at the knot...I begged you to stop, but you wouldn't. I could barely breathe. You were choking me!"

She was overwhelmed with emotion, and buried her face into his chest. Peter didn't dare mention that he, too, had the very same dream. His eyes shifted from the ribbon, to his hands, to the shadows on her neck around the ribbon.

Marks?

Or a trick of the light?

Their wedding day arrived, and Peter secretly wondered if this would be the day he waited for. But as she walked down the aisle in her glowing white dress, the dark black velvet circled her neck as it always did.

After several hours of eating, drinking, laughing and dancing with friends, the couple rode in a coach to the honeymoon suite at the finest hotel in town. Both bride and groom were drunk, and in love, kissing each other with no care for the coachman, ready to take each other in.

Peter excused himself for a shower as his new wife made herself comfortable in their extravagant suite. He returned to find her laying across the bed in a red velvet nightgown. The dark fabric emphasized her in the most perfect places. Her plump, juicy lips curved upwards invitingly, and her eyes glimmered from between falling black locs.

But still, he focused on the ribbon, and the building lust evaporated. If there were ever a time he wanted to see and smell and kiss the soft skin of her neck, it would be tonight!

She seemed to notice, and her smile dropped ever-so-slightly. He wouldn't risk spoiling the evening by asking her to remove it.

He climbed into bed with her - for the second time ever - and she held out her arms as she said, "Hello, husband."

He kissed her deeply and ran his hands up and down the soft fabric along her back. "I love you, my dearest."

"I love you, darling," she replied with a smile.

Their eyes locked, and the love was true. But he couldn't help it, and his attention drifted once again to the ribbon.

She sighed and sat back, sinking in disappointment. "Do you want to untie the bow?"

Peter lit up. He never thought the day would come when she would offer him what he desired most!

"After all this time...this is what you want of me?"

"Yes, my love," he said with a smirk.

Melody remained still. "Then do what you wish," she said softly.

Practically giddy, Peter began to forcefully finger the knot, but it was unyielding. He fetched a pair of scissors from the desk and returned with enthusiasm, sliding the cold metal blade between his new wife's velvety skin and the dark fabric, and snipped.

Then, he screamed. stumbling back from the bed and onto the floor...as her head toppled from her shoulders and rolled across the room.

www.ingramcontent.com/pod-product-compliance
Lightning Source LLC
LaVergne TN
LVHW031607060526
838201LV00063B/4767